OLIVER, AMANDA, AND GRANDMOTHER PIG

Jean Van Leeuwen

PICTURES BY

ANN SCHWENINGER

DIAL BOOKS FOR YOUNG READERS

NEW YORK

Dial easy-to-read

To Grandpa Sam and Grandpa Neil
and Grandma Dorothy

J.V.L.

For Ron

A.S.

Published by Dial Books for Young Readers
A Division of Penguin Books USA Inc.
2 Park Avenue
New York, New York 10016

Published simultaneously in Canada by
Fitzhenry & Whiteside Limited, Toronto

Library of Congress Cataloging in Publication Data
Van Leeuwen, Jean. Oliver, Amanda, and Grandmother Pig.
Summary: When Grandmother Pig comes for a visit,
Oliver and Amanda learn just how much fun it is
to have a grandmother in the house.
[1. Grandmothers—Fiction. 2. Pigs—Fiction.]
I. Schweninger, Ann, ill. II. Title.
PZ7.V3273Ol 1987   [E]   86-24326
E

First Hardcover Printing 1987
ISBN 0-8037-0361-9 (tr.)
ISBN 0-8037-0362-7 (lib. bdg.)
3 5 7 9 10 8 6 4 2

First Trade Paperback Printing 1990
ISBN 0-8037-0745-2 (ppr.)
1 3 5 7 9 10 8 6 4 2

The full-color artwork was prepared using carbon
pencil, colored pencils, and watercolor washes. It
was then color-separated and reproduced as red, blue,
yellow, and black halftones.

Reading Level 1.7

CONTENTS

THE VISIT

"Grandmother is coming to visit,"

said Mother.

"Oh, good," said Amanda.

"Grandmother and I will read books."

"Grandmother and I will build

skyscrapers," said Oliver.

"You can do lots of things

with Grandmother," said Mother.

"She will be here a whole week."

"Hooray!" said Oliver and Amanda.

Grandmother came after lunch.

She unpacked her suitcase.

She and Mother had

a cup of tea with honey.

Then she asked,

"What shall we do this afternoon?"

"Let's read books," said Amanda.

"Oh, dear," said Grandmother.

"I can't find my eyeglasses."

"Then let's build," said Oliver.

"I will get out the blocks."

"Oh, dear," said Grandmother.

"I can't sit on the floor.

My knees won't bend anymore.

Why don't we sing songs?"

Amanda climbed onto Grandmother's lap.

So did Oliver.

"You are getting too big to sit

on my lap together," said Grandmother.

"You will have to take turns."

"It's my turn first," said Oliver.

"No, mine," said Amanda.

Oliver pinched Amanda. Amanda cried.

She punched Oliver.

Grandmother covered her ears.

"This is too much noise," she said.

"I am going to take a nap."

Amanda went to find Mother.

"Grandmother is no fun," she said.

"She can't read or sit on the floor.

She thinks we are noisy.

And now she is taking a nap.

Grandmother is too old for naps."

"You are never too old for a nice nap,"

said Mother.

"But Grandmother is

too old for some things.

Like noise and bending over

and remembering where she put things.

At her house it is always quiet."

"Maybe she should go back

to her house," said Oliver.

"We can't be quiet for a whole week."

"Try," said Mother.

Oliver and Amanda tried.

At dinner they didn't fight

or spill their milk.

After dinner Amanda found

Grandmother's eyeglasses.

They were on top of the lampshade.

Grandmother read them a bedtime story.

In the night Amanda had a dream.

It was about monsters.

"Mother!" she called. "Father!"

But no one came.

Amanda started to cry.

"It's all right," said Grandmother.

"I am here."

She gave Amanda a handkerchief
and a big hug.

"Let's sing together," she said.

Amanda and Grandmother sang

quiet songs in the dark

until Amanda forgot her dream.

"Grandmother," she said.

"I am glad you are here."

"Me too," said Grandmother.

HELPING

Amanda woke up early.

Everyone else was sleeping.

She went to the kitchen

and Grandmother was there.

"I always wake up early,"

said Grandmother.

"Me too," said Amanda.

"And I feel lonely."

"Let's have breakfast together,"

said Grandmother.

Amanda set the table.

"I can't reach the cups," she said.

"They are up too high."

"I will help you," said Grandmother.

Grandmother cooked.

"I can't reach the pots," she said.

"They are down too low."

"I will help you," said Amanda.

They ate breakfast.

Still everyone else was sleeping.

"Let's go to the mailbox," said Amanda.

Grandmother and Amanda

walked down the road.

It was hard for Amanda

to walk so slowly.

"Look," said Grandmother. "Flowers."

"Let's pick some," said Amanda.

"I can't," said Grandmother.

"I will help you," said Amanda.

Grandmother helped Amanda
reach the mailbox.

Amanda helped Grandmother
carry the mail.

They put the mail and the flowers
on the kitchen table.

Still everyone else was sleeping.

"Let's read books," said Amanda.

"Good idea," said Grandmother.

"I can't read by myself," said Amanda.

"I don't know the words yet."

"I have trouble reading by myself too,"
said Grandmother.

"I can never find my eyeglasses."

Amanda found Grandmother's eyeglasses.

This time they were under her pillow.

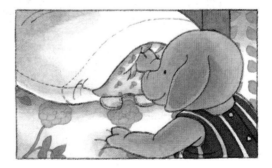

"It's good we have each other,"
said Grandmother.

They read four books,
and then Father got up.
"Good morning, early birds," he said.

23

"Grandmother and I have had breakfast," said Amanda.

"And we got the mail and picked flowers and read four books."

"You did all of that already?" said Father.

"Yes," said Amanda.

"I helped Grandmother,

and Grandmother helped me."

"That is nice," said Father.

"Grandmother," said Amanda.

"Can we be early birds again tomorrow?"

"I will meet you in the kitchen,"

said Grandmother,

"at seven o'clock."

BAD OLIVER

"Oh, dear," said Grandmother.

"I have lost my eyeglasses again.

I have looked everywhere."

"Look in the mirror," said Oliver.

"You are wearing them."

"Why, so I am!" said Grandmother.

Oliver and Amanda laughed.

"Grandmother is so silly,"

said Oliver.

"I am going to play a trick on her.

I am going to hide her eyeglasses."

"You better not," said Amanda.

"You will get in trouble."

"No, I won't," said Oliver.

While Grandmother drank a cup of tea,

Oliver took her eyeglasses.

He put them on his tiger.

"Grandmother will never find
her eyeglasses this time," he said.
"Has anyone seen my eyeglasses?"
asked Grandmother.
"I bet Oliver can find them,"
said Amanda.
"No, I can't," said Oliver.

Everyone looked

but no one could find them.

"What will I do?" said Grandmother.

"I can't see without my eyeglasses."

"Oliver," said Amanda.

"Are you sure you can't find them?"

Everyone looked at Oliver.

He went to his room and got his tiger.

"Here they are!" he said.

"Oliver," said Father.

"That was a bad thing to do.

Go to your room and stay there."

"It was only a trick," said Oliver.

"Go!" said Father.

Oliver sat in his room all alone.

He could hear everyone talking.

He could smell dinner cooking.

But no one called him to have some.

There was a knock on the door.

It was Grandmother.

She sat down next to Oliver on his bed.

"When I was little," she said,

"I once did something very bad."

"As bad as me?" Oliver asked.

"Worse," said Grandmother.

"My mother always used to sit
in her rocking chair and sew.
One day I took a pincushion
and put it on her chair."
"What happened?" asked Oliver.
"Well," said Grandmother.
"She sat down, and then she screamed
and got up again very fast."

Oliver laughed.

"Was your mother angry?" he asked.

"I was sent to my room

without any dinner," said Grandmother.

"Just like me," said Oliver.

"Bad Grandmother."

"I never did it again though,"

said Grandmother.

"I will never hide your eyeglasses

again," said Oliver.

"Good," said Grandmother.

"I think there might be some dinner

waiting for you downstairs."

"Would you sit with me

while I eat it?" asked Oliver.

"I would," said Grandmother.

THUNDER AND LIGHTNING

"Good-bye," said Mother.

"I am going to the store."

"Who will take care of us?"

asked Amanda.

"Grandmother," said Mother.

"You know she always took care of me

when I was little."

"But maybe she has forgotten
how to do it," said Oliver.
"There are some things
you never forget how to do,"
said Mother.
Oliver and Amanda played outside.

"Look at the sky," said Amanda.

"It's nighttime already."

"It can't be," said Oliver.

"We just had lunch."

"Oliver! Amanda!" called Grandmother.

"Come inside. It is going to rain."

Amanda put away her wagon.

"What was that noise?" she asked.

"Thunder," said Grandmother.

"I'm scared of thunder," said Amanda.

"It sounds like a monster growling."

"I don't like lightning," said Oliver.

"Come," said Grandmother.

"I will tell you a story."

"About when you were little?"

asked Oliver.

"Yes," said Grandmother.

She told them a funny story

about going on a picnic

with her six sisters and five brothers.

"Grandmother," said Amanda.

"The thunder is getting louder."

"If we sing songs," said Grandmother,

"maybe we won't hear it."

They sang loud songs.

Oliver beat on his drum.

But they could still hear thunder

and rain beating on the roof.

"I'm scared," said Amanda.

"I want this storm to stop right now."

"It won't stop until it's over,"

said Grandmother.

"But I know how

we can stop listening to it.

We will need a lot of pillows."

Oliver and Amanda got pillows

from their rooms

and pillows from the couch.

"More than that," said Grandmother.

They got pillows

from Mother and Father's room

and pillows from the big chair.

"That may be enough," said Grandmother.

"Now cover your ears with pillows."

Oliver put two pillows on each ear.

Amanda covered herself with pillows.

"I can't hear a thing," she said.

She couldn't breathe either.

She took one off.

"Hey, watch out," said Oliver.

He threw the pillow at her.

Amanda threw it back.

It hit Grandmother.

"Pillow fight!" said Oliver.

Grandmother and Oliver and Amanda
laughed and threw pillows
until they were all tired out.

"Listen," said Grandmother.

Outside everything was quiet.

"The storm is over," said Amanda.

"That was a bad storm," said Oliver.

"But you took care of us.

You didn't forget how."

"There are some things
you never forget how to do,"
said Grandmother.

GOOD-BYE

Grandmother was pǎcking up.

Tomorrow she was going home.

Amanda helped Grandmother.

She reached things for her

and carried things for her

and sat on her suitcase to close it.

"That was hard work," said Grandmother.

"I need a nap before dinner."

Amanda went to the kitchen.

Mother was cooking.

"What are you making?" she asked.

"A good-bye dinner for Grandmother,"

said Mother.

"It has all of her favorites:

liver and onions and lima beans."

"Liver?" said Oliver. "Lima beans?

Grandmother's favorites

are not my favorites."

"Can we make something

for Grandmother too?" asked Amanda.

"What would it be?" asked Mother.

"A good-bye cake," said Amanda.

"It will be all pink."

"I like chocolate cake," said Oliver.

"Why don't you make a

chocolate and pink cake?" said Mother.

Oliver and Amanda mixed up the cake.

Mother baked it.

On top they wrote with icing: GOOD-BYE.

When Grandmother got up from her nap

she said, "Something smells good."

"It is your good-bye dinner,"

said Oliver.

Grandmother liked her good-bye dinner.

Oliver and Amanda didn't.

Except for the cake.

"We made it ourselves," said Amanda.

"Look what it says on top,"

said Oliver.

"Oh, dear," said Grandmother.

"Where have my eyeglasses gone?"

"I will find them," said Amanda.

She looked all over.

"You won't believe it," she said.

"They were in the wastebasket."

"I will miss having you to find
my eyeglasses," said Grandmother.

"I will miss being early birds together," said Amanda.

"I will miss hearing stories about when you were little," said Oliver.

"And singing songs," said Amanda.

"Do you know what I will miss the most?" said Grandmother.

"What?" asked Oliver.

"Your noise," said Grandmother.

"It is too quiet at my house."

"Soon we will come to visit you," said Oliver.

"And we will make lots of noise."

"Oh, good," said Grandmother.

"Now who would like a slice of cake?"

"Me!" said Oliver and Amanda.

And they all had big slices

of Grandmother's good-bye cake.